Fairy Blossoms

Marigold and the Missing Firefly

BOOK 4

Fairy Blossoms

Marigold and the Missing Firefly

By Suzanne Williams
Illustrated by Fiona Sansom

■ HARPERTROPHY®
AN IMPRINT OF HARPERCOLLINS*PUBLISHERS*

HarperTrophy® is a registered trademark
of HarperCollins Publishers.

Fairy Blossoms #4: Marigold and the Missing Firefly
Text copyright © 2008 by Suzanne Williams
Illustrations copyright © 2008 by Fiona Sansom
www.harpercollinschildrens.com

Library of Congress Cataloging-in-Publication Data is available.
ISBN 978-0-06-113941-3

Typography by Andrea Vandergrift
❖
First Edition

To Jenny, my wonderful daughter-in-law

Contents

1

A Present

One warm, sunny morning at Cloverleaf Cottage, Marigold woke up late. She fluttered down from her flower bed to the ground below. Next to her flower's stem she was surprised to find a large package wrapped in shiny gold paper. She checked the label. Her family had sent it. "Goody!" Marigold exclaimed. She loved presents as much as she loved food.

Holes had been punched in the top of the package, and Marigold wondered what could be inside. Quickly, she tore off the paper and opened the box. Inside was another, slightly smaller box. This box had a lid, and holes had been punched in it, too.

Marigold lifted the lid. To her delight, a firefly with glossy black wings and a red head looked up at her from the box. He flickered his green light in greeting. Then he stretched his wings and stood up on six shaky legs.

"You're a cute little fellow," said Marigold. At home she and her sister had often had fireflies as pets.

The firefly nuzzled Marigold's hand. She patted his head. "I think I'll call you Flash."

As if to show that he liked his new name, Flash winked his green light on and off again. Then he climbed out of his box, turned in a circle, and looked all around the flower garden where the junior fairies slept.

"You'll like it here," said Marigold. "Shall I show you around?"

Flash bobbed his head as if to say yes.

"Then come with me," said Marigold.

Still dressed in pajamas, she fluttered her wings and flew up above the garden. In a moment Flash caught up with her. When they passed over a rosebush, she pointed to a

large pink rose at the top of the bush. "That's where my best friend, Rose, sleeps," she told him. Then she pointed out the flower beds of the other six junior fairies. Her friends were at breakfast now. Marigold would have been there too, if she hadn't woken up late.

After they flew over the flower garden, Marigold took Flash down to the golden bridge that crossed over the stream in front of Cloverleaf Cottage. The sparkly jewels that decorated the bridge's rails seemed to excite Flash. He zipped back and forth over the rails several times, stopping to peer closely at the diamonds, emeralds, and rubies.

On the other side of the bridge, a path bordered with pink-blossomed clover led into the village. "Stay on this side of the bridge," Marigold told Flash. "We'll explore the village another day."

Flash seemed happy to do as she asked. He stuck close to Marigold's side as they left the bridge and fluttered over the cottage's front lawn to land on the clover-covered roof. From there Marigold pointed out the stables, where three winged ponies were kept, and the forest behind. She would've taken Flash inside the cottage to meet the other fairies next, but it was almost time for class. So instead they flew back to Marigold's flower bed. Quickly, she waved her wand and changed her pajamas into a dress.

"I wish I could take you with me," said Marigold. "But I don't think Mistress Lily would allow pets in class. Maybe you should stay in your box until I get back."

Flash's wings went all droopy, but he dutifully crawled into his box. "Don't be sad," said Marigold. "I'll be back soon." Flash must have understood because he bobbed his

head, then lay down in a corner of the l
Marigold set the lid on top. As she flew to
the cottage, she hoped Flash wouldn't get *too*
lonely while she was gone.

2

Transformations

Once inside the cottage, Marigold flew up to the balcony. "Phew," she said as she dropped into her seat beside Rose. "I was afraid I might be late."

Rose ran a hand through her jet-black ringlets, then settled her silver tiara more firmly on top of her head. "How come you weren't at breakfast? Did you oversleep?"

"Yes," said Marigold. She glanced over her

shoulder at Rose. "And when I fluttered down from my flower bed, I . . ." Catching a glimpse of her wings, she exclaimed, "Oh my!" They were covered with a design of half-moons and stars that matched the pajamas she'd worn last night but definitely didn't go with her strawberry-colored silk dress.

"Excuse me," said Marigold. "I forgot to fix my wings." Drawing out her wand, she fussed around with different designs. Finally she settled on filmy white wings covered with tiny multicolored sparkles. "That's better," she said.

Rose gave her a thumbs-up.

Their teacher flew to the balcony railing at the front of the classroom. Marigold would have to tell Rose about Flash later.

Mistress Lily smoothed down her beautiful blue gown. "Today we will begin learning to transform objects," she said. "As

fairy helpers, you will find this a very useful skill."

"Goody!" cried Marigold, unable to contain her excitement.

Everyone laughed, including Mistress Lily. She had a tinkly laugh, like a silver bell.

Marigold blushed. She'd wanted to become a fairy helper for a very long time—for most of her nine years, in fact.

Mistress Lily looped a strand of golden hair behind her ear. "You'll need to choose objects carefully," she said. "They should be similar in some way to whatever you're trying to create."

Heather raised her hand. She and her two sisters, Holly and Hyacinth, were triplets. They dressed identically and their fair hair was always braided, then pinned across the tops of their heads.

"Yes?" asked Mistress Lily.

"Is that why a scooped-out pumpkin makes a good coach?" Heather asked.

"Exactly," said Mistress Lily.

Now Holly raised her hand. "You could use a pumpkin to make a cradle or a bassinet, couldn't you?"

Marigold caught Rose's eye. Rose arched an eyebrow. Everyone in class knew the triplets were baby crazy. They wanted to become birth fairies so that they could bestow blessings on babies.

"Yes," Mistress Lily agreed. "I suppose you could use pumpkins for that purpose."

The mention of pumpkins reminded Marigold of the pumpkin spice bars she'd eaten for dinner last night. She'd *loved* them. Her stomach growled. It was too bad she'd missed breakfast.

Mistress Lily grabbed a book from a desk and held it up in the air. "Quick!" she said.

"Put on your thinking caps. What could we make from this object?"

Marigold's brain froze. It was a familiar feeling and happened whenever she felt called upon to give a fast answer.

"A door?" suggested Rose.

"Why?" asked Mistress Lily. "How are doors similar to books?"

"Both are rectangles and both can be opened and closed."

"Good one, Rose," Marigold whispered, wishing she were even half as clever as her friend.

"Excellent," said Mistress Lily. "Anyone else?"

The triplets had put their heads together. Now they all looked up. "A chest of drawers," said Hyacinth.

"For a baby's room," added Holly.

"Same shapes," Heather said. "And they

open and close too, just like a door."

"Very good," Mistress Lily said. "How about the rest of you? Any other ideas?"

"A suitcase," said Poppy. "Same shapes again. They also open and close. And they can both take you places."

Mistress Lily smiled. "That's going to be hard to top." She looked around the room. "Marigold," she said. "Give us another idea."

Marigold panicked. "A cake?" Because she was hungry, it was the first thing that popped into her head.

"A cake?" Mistress Lily repeated.

"A—a *birthday* cake," said Marigold. "One of those big rectangular ones." But for the life of her, she couldn't think how else a cake was like a book. Feeling stupid, she stared down at the floor and hoped Mistress Lily would call on someone else.

"A birthday cake," her teacher repeated. "Has anyone ever eaten food that's been transformed from other objects?" she asked.

"I have," said Violet, who was so shy she rarely said anything in class. She looked at Marigold with large brown eyes. "Food made from objects tastes awful."

"Like cardboard," Daisy agreed.

Marigold blushed. Now her stupid idea seemed even *more* stupid.

Fortunately, Poppy spoke up and everyone turned toward her. "That reminds me of something that happened to me."

"And what's that?" asked Mistress Lily.

"One day when I was walking in the woods near my home, I came upon a man," said Poppy, warming to her story. "Before he could see me, I turned myself into a blackberry to hide." Poppy paused. "Unfortunately, the man had wandered into the woods to gather blackberries. Before I could change back, he picked me and ate me!"

"Heavens!" Mistress Lily exclaimed. "How did you escape?"

Poppy's eyes twinkled. "Luckily, the man swallowed me whole. I tickled his insides until he started to laugh. When he opened his mouth wide, I hopped out and flew away."

The fairies giggled.

Feeling better now, Marigold said, "I bet *he* was surprised."

Poppy nodded. "You should've seen the look on his face."

A few minutes later classwork began when Mistress Lily passed out pictures of objects.

Marigold's picture was of an acorn.

"You have until the end of class—about ten minutes—to list as many ideas as you can for transforming your object," Mistress Lily told everyone.

Only ten minutes? Marigold stared at her picture, but perhaps because she was growing more and more hungry, all she could think of were acorn pancakes. She couldn't write that down—pancakes were *food*.

Think about the shape *of the object*, she reminded herself. Acorns were round. *Ball*, she thought. But then she was stuck again. She glanced at Rose and saw that she had already scribbled a half page of ideas for *her* object.

Sighing, Marigold stared at her acorn picture. Finally she wrote down *drum*. And just as class ended, she added *barrel*. Luckily, Mistress Lily didn't ask the class to turn in their lists.

"I need to ask Mistress Lily a question about the lesson," Rose said as Marigold got ready to leave. "See you at lunch in a few minutes."

Too late, Marigold remembered that she still hadn't told Rose—or anyone else, for that matter—about Flash. Well, the junior fairies could all meet him at lunch. Marigold zipped over the balcony and out the door to her flower bed. She could hardly wait to see him again!

3

Meeting Flash

As soon as Marigold lifted the lid, Flash stood up in his box. He stretched his legs and wings. "Did you miss me?" asked Marigold, petting him. Flash bobbed his head in answer. Then he nuzzled Marigold's hand.

"Come on," said Marigold. "I want you to meet my friends." Flash left his box and flew beside Marigold to the cottage. As they

entered, Marigold called out, "Hey, everyone!
Come see my pet firefly!"

Rose, Daisy, and Poppy were already seated
at the dining room table, but Violet and the

triplets had been relaxing on thistledown cushions in the sitting area. Now they all hurried to gather around Marigold. Flash scooted closer to her and hid his head in the folds of her skirt.

"Don't be shy," said Marigold. "These are my friends. You'll like them." Flash peeked out at the fairies and flickered his green light. "He's saying hello," said Marigold.

"Where did you find him?" asked Rose.

"I didn't," said Marigold. "My family sent him. Flash was a present."

"That's a good name for a firefly," said Violet.

"He's adorable," said Holly. "Almost as cute as a baby."

Bink walked out of the kitchen. The brownie servant carried a tray of blackberry scones. They were a specialty of the cottage's new hobgoblin baker, Hobart. "Goody!"

Marigold exclaimed. "I'm starved!"

The fairies sat down around the table on toadstools covered with tasseled satin cloth. Flash settled at Marigold's feet. He peered at the chandelier above, fascinated by the light or the tinkling sound that the dangling crystals made.

Bink smiled at the firefly as he set the tray on top of the white lace tablecloth. "I bet you'd like something to eat too," he said. "Shall I bring you a nice cup of peach tea with lots of sugar?"

"Thanks," said Marigold. "I'm sure Flash would like that." She reached for the tray and piled six scones on her plate.

Bink brushed back a lock of reddish-brown hair that had fallen over one eye and grinned. "Maybe I should've brought you your very own tray."

Marigold blushed at his teasing. "I shouldn't

have missed breakfast," she said. "Now I'm *super* hungry."

"Good thing Hobart made a double batch," said Bink. "I'll bring some more with Flash's tea."

As Bink returned to the kitchen, Daisy asked, "Where are you going to keep Flash?"

Marigold swallowed a delicious bite of the buttery scone. Blackberry jam oozed out and she bent to let Flash suck it off her fingers.

"When he's not with me, he can stay in the box he arrived in," she said. "Later, when he gets used to being here, I'll let him fly free."

Daisy and Poppy began to talk about class. "I hope we start practicing with real objects soon," said Poppy.

"It'll probably be easy for you," Marigold said, "since you can shape-shift." Not many flower fairies could do that without lots of practice, but Poppy was half pixie. Pixies were expert shape-shifters.

Poppy shrugged. "Changing my *own* shape isn't the same as changing the shapes of other things. But you could be right."

It was almost time for class again. Marigold offered Flash a few scone crumbs, but he seemed more interested in the sugary saucer of peach tea that Bink had brought him.

"Ready to go?" Rose asked.

Marigold wiped her mouth with her napkin. "I'll catch up with you. I need to take Flash back to his box first."

But Flash didn't *want* to go back into his box. He hopped out before Marigold could lower the lid and crawled away, his wings all droopy. "I guess you don't want to stay in your box, do you?" said Marigold.

In answer, Flash flew to the top of Marigold's bed and lay down in the center. "Oh, all right." Marigold sighed. "But if I leave you here, you have to promise to stay put. You can't go flying off on your own."

Flash bobbed his head to show that he understood. Then he blinked his light on and off five times fast to say how happy he was that he didn't have to go back into his box.

Marigold hugged Flash. He nuzzled her cheek, and his wings made a soft whirring noise. "I won't be gone long," she said. Then she flew back to the cottage. As she fluttered up to the balcony, Marigold hoped that letting Flash wait in the garden had been the right decision.

The First Practice

Mistress Lily gave each fairy a shiny silver thimble. "We'll practice transforming small things first," she said. She pulled out her wand—a silver one that sparkled with dark blue sapphires. "Remember what we talked about this morning?" she asked. "What could you make from a thimble? Any ideas?"

Violet raised her hand timidly. "A bowl?"

"Good idea, Violet," Mistress Lily said. "Watch me first, please. Then we'll all try."

Mistress Lily set a thimble on top of her desk. Eyeing it carefully, she tapped the thimble with the tip of her wand. Instantly, it transformed into a beautiful silver bowl.

The fairies oohed and aahed. "Cool!" Daisy exclaimed.

Mistress Lily smiled. "It's important to let your mind form a clear picture of whatever you're trying to create before you tap your object. Get the size, shape, and details firmly in mind. You must also be careful to tap gently. Otherwise, your object could explode."

Explode? Marigold's eyes widened. She sure didn't want *that* to happen.

"Do our wands always need to touch the objects to transform them?" Rose asked.

"Excellent question," said Mistress Lily.

"No, your wand doesn't actually need to touch the object. But unless you have perfect aim, it's best to tap. Otherwise it's easy to transform the wrong thing. Aiming across long distances is especially difficult."

Heather raised her hand. "Do we have to make a bowl, or can we make something else?"

"You may decide," said Mistress Lily. "Just remember that whatever you choose should be similar to a thimble in some small way." She paused. "Any more questions?"

Poppy drummed her fingers on top of her desk. "Yes. Can we start now?"

Mistress Lily laughed. "You may."

Marigold stared at her thimble. Before she could even begin to think what to make, she heard a small explosion. A cloud of glittering silver dust rose into the air.

"Petal rot!" Poppy exclaimed.

Everyone laughed.

Mistress Lily handed Poppy another thimble. "Try again."

Daisy tapped her thimble and a canoe suddenly stretched sideways across her desk

and two others, knocking Holly's and
Violet's thimbles to the floor.

"Oh, dear!" Daisy cried.

Mistress Lily aimed her wand at Daisy's

canoe and shrank it. "You'll want to think about the size of the object you're creating the next time," she said gently.

Rose transformed her thimble into a beautiful silver bell. She picked it up and rang it. The tone was sweet and clear. "What do you think?" she asked Marigold.

"I *love* it," she said. "You're so clever, Rose!"

"Thanks." Rose glanced at Marigold's thimble. "What are you going to make?"

Marigold shrugged. "I haven't decided yet." She didn't want to admit that she was having trouble coming up with ideas.

"Hey, guess what I made!" Heather crowed.

"Don't tell me," said Poppy. "A cradle?"

"That's right!" Heather exclaimed. "How did you know?"

Poppy grinned. "It was just a wild guess."

Think! Marigold scolded herself. But, as usual, her brain had stalled. Soon class would be over and she'd be the only junior fairy with a thimble still sitting on top of her desk. *Just* do *something. Anything!* she thought.

"Five more minutes, everyone," said Mistress Lily.

Marigold panicked. She was about to give up when at last an idea leaped into her head. Without pausing to think it through, she pulled out her amber-studded gold wand and tapped her thimble.

Instantly, an ugly metal blob appeared. Marigold groaned. She had wanted to make a vase.

"Trouble?" asked Rose. She squinted at the blob. "What is it?"

Marigold frowned. "It's a *mistake*." How could she be so good at designing dresses, but so awful at this? It just didn't seem fair.

But then she thought of Flash, waiting for her on top of her flower bed, and she felt better.

Before class ended, Mistress Lily showed the fairies how to turn their creations back into thimbles. Marigold was glad to reverse the spell. She tapped the ugly metal blob three times, and it became a thimble again.

"May we keep them?" Marigold asked. She could fill the thimble with the sugary peach tea that Flash had liked so much.

"You may," said Mistress Lily.

"Goody!" Marigold exclaimed. Flash would *love* his new bowl.

"Want to do something with Flash and me?" Marigold asked Rose as they left the classroom.

"Sure," said Rose. "I'd like that."

"I'll go get him," said Marigold. "We'll meet you down by the bridge." They only had half an hour before their last class of the day. It wouldn't be enough time to fly into the village, but at least Flash could stretch his wings.

Marigold was relieved to see that Flash was

still lying on top of her flower bed. As soon as he saw her, he perked up and flickered his light in greeting. She hugged him. "What a good firefly you are," she said. "Want to go to the bridge and see Rose?"

Flash leaped off Marigold's flower and began to fly circles around her.

Marigold laughed. "Let's go, then."

Flash stuck close to her side as they left the garden, crossed the cottage lawn, and flew down to the bridge. Rose had taken off her shoes and sat dipping her toes in the stream. Seeing the sparkly jewels again, Flash was too excited to greet her. Like before, he zipped back and forth over the rails, stopping to peer closely at the diamonds, emeralds, and rubies.

Rose and Marigold smiled at each other, amused. When Flash finally tired of looking at the rails, he settled between the two fairies, laying his head in Marigold's lap. While Marigold stroked his folded wings, her thoughts turned to class. She frowned. "You know that ugly metal blob I made? It was supposed to be a vase."

Rose shrugged. "You just needed more

time to get it right. Next time you'll do better."

"You think so?" said Marigold, feeling more cheerful. "Thanks."

When it was almost time for class again, Rose flew to the cottage while Marigold dropped Flash off at her flower.

"See you after class," she said, giving him a quick hug. As she fluttered away, she glanced back over her shoulder. Flash lifted a wing, as if he was waving good-bye. Marigold smiled fondly and waved back. She couldn't believe how quickly she'd grown to love Flash. And she knew he felt the same way about her.

5

What Rose Made

This time Mistress Lily gave each junior fairy a sunflower seed to practice on. "Remember to tap gently so that your seed won't explode," she reminded the fairies.

"I'm not taking any chances," Poppy said. She placed her sunflower seed on top of her desk. Standing a foot away, she aimed her gold and emerald wand. In an instant, her desk transformed into something resembling a gigantic, lopsided cart. "Petal rot!" she cried as her sunflower seed slid to the floor. "I missed!"

With three quick taps from her wand, Poppy returned her desk to normal. "I guess that's why it's not a good idea to aim from a distance," she said.

"Especially if your aim isn't very good," Rose whispered to Marigold.

But Marigold was too busy staring at her sunflower seed to reply. As usual, she was having trouble thinking what to make. Finally, just before the end of class, a picture of a giant sunflower-seed cookie popped into her head. *No food,* she reminded herself. But how about a cookie *jar?*

Doing her best to hold on to the picture, Marigold tapped her seed with her wand.

Instantly, it turned into an attractive ceramic cookie jar with a sunflower-shaped lid.

"I did it!" she exclaimed in surprise. But when she picked it up, she saw that the jar

43

had no bottom. All the same, it was an improvement over her vase.

As soon as class was over, Marigold flew straight to her flower. Flash was waiting for her and winked his light joyfully the moment he saw her. During dinner, he sat beside her toadstool and drank sugary peach tea from the thimble she'd saved for him. He sipped slowly and didn't spill a drop.

"He's a very dainty eater, isn't he?" Rose said with approval.

"Yes, he is," said Marigold proudly. She patted Flash on the head, and he seemed to smile at her.

The other fairies wanted to play with Flash, so after dinner they made up a game. The fairies spread out around the cottage and took turns calling to Flash. As he flew from one fairy to the next, his light flickered happily.

"He's so cute!" said Heather. She reached out to hug him as he flew by, but Flash dodged her arms.

Poppy grinned. "Smart, too."

By the end of the game, Flash had worn himself out with all his flying around. The sun hadn't yet set when Marigold took him back to her flower. She covered him with a petal and sang him a tender fairy lullaby. "Sleep tight," she whispered, kissing him lightly on the top of his head. His light flickered dimly.

Marigold flew back to the cottage. Bink had finished clearing away the dinner things and was chatting with Poppy and Daisy in the sitting area. Daisy waved at Marigold, then patted the thistledown cushion next to her. "Come join us," she said.

Marigold did, and soon the four were talking and laughing about their last adventure—which had ended happily with Hobart's coming to live and work in the kitchen at Cloverleaf Cottage.

"Where's Rose?" Marigold asked after a while.

Poppy shrugged. "You know how hard she works. She said she wanted more transformation practice before tomorrow's class."

"That's what I should be doing," Marigold said guiltily. She excused herself and flew up to the balcony to search for Rose. But Rose wasn't in the classroom. Marigold flew down to the main floor again. Maybe Rose had gone outside to practice. It was dusk by now, but as soon as Marigold stepped out the front door, she spotted Rose down by the bridge. "Yoo-hoo!" Marigold called out to her. "I've been looking for you!"

Rose waved to her. "Come see what I made!"

Marigold flew to the bridge, and Rose showed her an oval-shaped, glossy black box. On the lid was a large red dot.

"Pretty," said Marigold.

Rose handed it to her. "Open it."

"Okay." Marigold lifted the lid on its hinges. The inside of the box was bright green, but the box itself was empty.

"Listen to it," said Rose. "See if you can hear anything."

Puzzled, Marigold brought the box up to

her ear. For a second, she thought she heard a soft whirring sound, but it was probably just the wind in the trees. "*Should* I hear something?" she asked.

Rose laughed. "It's supposed to be a music

box. I transformed it from a twig. I don't know why it didn't turn out as well as my silver bell. And the colors aren't what I imagined at all."

Marigold grinned. It was nice to know that, as clever as Rose was, not everything she did turned out perfectly.

"What are you going to do with the box?" asked Marigold.

"I don't know," said Rose. "Would you like to have it?"

"May I?"

Rose nodded.

"Thanks," said Marigold. "I was thinking it might make a good bed for Flash." He liked her bed, of course, but it would be a bit crowded for two. She thought he'd like sleeping in this pretty box—with the lid open, of course.

The sky was almost dark when Marigold

and Rose returned to the cottage. They passed Bink, who was on his way to the stables to feed the winged ponies, and waved to him. Inside, Violet and the triplets had joined Daisy and Poppy on cushions in the sitting area. Marigold showed everyone Rose's box.

"Pretty," said Heather.

"Black and red," said Violet. "Just like Flash."

Marigold nodded. "Rose transformed it from a twig," she told them. "She's letting me have it for Flash's bed." Tactfully, she didn't mention that Rose had actually been trying to make a music box. "Speaking of Flash," Marigold said, "I'd better go check on him." She didn't like leaving him on his own for too long. Besides, she was tired and ready for bed herself.

With Rose's box cradled in her arms,

Marigold left the cottage and flew to the garden. "Wake up, Flash!" she called as she approached her flower bed. "I've brought you something!"

But Flash was gone.

6

The Search

Marigold set Rose's box on the ground. Where could Flash be? He'd been so good about staying on her flower bed that she'd stopped thinking he might wander off. Besides, he'd been almost asleep when she left him. But what if he'd woken up and gone to look for her? Circling above the garden, she called his name over and over.

Flash's green light didn't answer her back.

Marigold bit her lip. Beginning to worry, she flew to the cottage. Her friends were still inside. "Could you help me look for Flash?" Marigold asked. "I can't find him anywhere."

Moments later, all eight of the junior fairies were searching for Flash. Their wands glowed, helping to light the dark sky, as they crisscrossed the lawn and flew around the cottage, the garden, and the stables. Poppy and Daisy even searched *inside* the cottage, in case Flash had managed to get in without anyone noticing. Down by the bridge, Marigold thought she glimpsed Flash's green light. But it was only an emerald sparkling in the moonlight on one of the rails.

The fairies searched for an hour, but without success. Finally Rose said gently, "I don't think we're going to find Flash tonight,

Marigold." She put her arm around Marigold's shoulders. "He'll probably turn up on his own by morning."

"Do you think so?" Marigold asked, her voice full of hope.

"Sure," said Rose, but her eyes didn't quite meet Marigold's.

Marigold *wanted* to believe her. But what if something horrible had happened? She imagined Flash wandering around in the dark, lost and cold. What if he'd flown as far away as the forest behind the cottage? The woods were a dangerous place at night. Why, he could be swallowed up by a bat! Just thinking about it, her throat tightened and tears welled up in her eyes.

The fairies flew to the garden. Rose squeezed Marigold's shoulder. "See you in the morning," she said softly before fluttering off to bed.

Marigold changed her dress into pajamas. She lay on top of her flower, but she couldn't sleep. Her brain swirled with thoughts of Flash and she longed for him to nuzzle her cheek. After tossing and turning for several more minutes, Marigold slipped out of bed. The pretty oval box Rose had made from a twig lay on the ground, right under her flower.

Marigold picked up the box and clasped it to her chest. Then she took it to bed with her. Strangely enough, there was something comforting about the glossy black box with the big red dot. As she curled herself around it, Marigold began to feel sleepy. Shutting her eyes, she could almost imagine that Flash was beside her. When she rested her head against the box, she could even imagine she heard the soft whir of his wings. Wherever Flash was, Marigold hoped he was

all right. Holding on to that thought, at last
she drifted off to sleep.

When she awoke the next morning, it was
a few seconds before Marigold remembered
that Flash was gone. As she lay with her eyes

still closed, she thought again that she heard his wings whirring. She opened her eyes and sat up quickly. "Flash?"

But the firefly wasn't there. Only Rose's box lay next to her. Sighing, Marigold left the box on top of her flower and flew to the ground. She ran her wand over herself to change from pajamas to a skirt and blouse. Usually she took more care with her clothing and decorated her wings to match, but not today. Today it just didn't seem to matter.

During breakfast, everyone was super nice to her. "Sit here," said Poppy, patting the chair between her and Daisy.

"Let me pour you some tea," said Rose.

"I heard about Flash," said Bink. "I'm awfully sorry." Without even asking, and with no teasing at all, he piled *eight* acorn pancakes topped with raspberry syrup and

whipped cream on top of Marigold's plate.
But of course, she had no appetite. She
picked at the pancakes and only managed a
few small bites.

On the way up to the balcony for class, Heather swooped between Marigold and Rose. "If you let them know what happened, maybe your parents will send you a *new* firefly," she said.

"I don't *want* a new firefly!" Marigold snapped. "I only want Flash!"

Heather's eyes widened. "S-sorry," she stuttered. "I didn't mean to upset you." Fluttering faster, she flew to catch up with her sisters.

Rose glanced at Marigold. "I bet Heather's never had a pet. She doesn't understand how special they become, even in a short while." She paused. "I had a pet caterpillar once. It used to climb on my shoulder and nibble my ear. But after it became a butterfly, it flew away. I was heartbroken. I thought it would stay forever."

Was Rose trying to say she'd changed her

mind—that she thought Flash wouldn't be back after all? Marigold brushed at a tear with the back of her hand. Flash would turn up. He *had* to!

7

Chirp!

Mistress Lily decided to take the fairies outside to practice their transformation skills. It was a windy day, and a strong breeze whipped her hair across her face. "Look around you," she said, as they stood on the front lawn of the cottage. "Find an object that seems a good match for something you want to make."

Marigold had to hold her arms at her sides
to keep her skirt from billowing up. She
gazed toward a tree at the edge of the lawn.
Suddenly, from the corner of her eye, she saw

something green move. Her heart leaped for joy. "Flash!" she called out.

But it was only a leaf blowing in the wind.

The disappointment was just too much. Marigold burst into tears while the other fairies looked on in dismay.

"Why, whatever is the matter, Marigold?" Mistress Lily asked.

Marigold was crying too hard to answer.

Rose put her arm around Marigold in an effort to comfort her, while the rest of the fairies explained about Flash.

"Oh, dear," said Mistress Lily when they'd finished telling the story. "I'm sorry you've lost your pet, Marigold. No wonder you feel sad! Would you like to sit on the porch with Rose until you feel a little better?"

Still sniffling, Marigold nodded. Rose guided her to the porch and they sat down together. Side by side, they stared out over the lawn, watching the other fairies practice. Violet aimed her wand toward a bush. With a loud *chirp!* something fell to the ground.

"Oh, no!" cried Violet.

Rose raised an eyebrow. "I wonder what she hit?"

She and Marigold watched as Violet searched under the bush. In a few seconds, she pulled out a lumpy yellow hat. A few black-and-white feathers stuck out of the

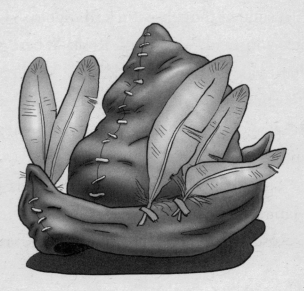

brim. Violet tapped the hat with her wand three times. Instantly, a startled-looking goldfinch appeared. She gave Violet a beady-eyed look and let out a long string of chirps.

Marigold couldn't help laughing. "She's scolding you!" she called out.

Violet blushed. "It was an accident. I didn't know she was in the bush." After a moment, the bird hopped away, and Violet flew off to practice somewhere else.

A sudden thought struck Marigold. "That box you made yesterday, Rose. Where was that twig you transformed?"

"On top of one of the bridge rails," said Rose. "I was crossing the lawn when I saw it."

"So you didn't see the twig up close?" asked Marigold. "Wasn't it also dusk by then?"

Rose shrugged. "I suppose. But I have

excellent aim. I know my spell hit it."

"Yes, I'm sure that it did too." Marigold pictured the box. Glossy black like Flash's wings, it had a red dot on the lid that matched the top of his head. And inside, the box was the exact same green as the light he gave off. She jumped up from the porch. "I know what happened to Flash. I know where he is!"

Rose stared at her in surprise. "You do?"

"Follow me!" said Marigold. "Hurry!"

They flew to the garden. As they approached her flower bed, Marigold told Rose what she thought had happened.

Rose's hands flew to her mouth. "So you think it wasn't a twig I saw? You think that I—"

"—transformed Flash?" Marigold nodded. "Violet's hat gave me the idea. Even if the goldfinch hadn't chirped, the hat was yellow,

67

like the bird, not green like the bush."

"I can't believe it!" Rose exclaimed. "How awful!"

"You can change him back to his real self in a jiffy," said Marigold as they swooped toward her bed. "All you have to do is tap three . . ."

She stopped short and stared at her flower in disbelief. Just like Flash, Rose's box had vanished!

8

Cookies

"Are you sure you left it on top of your flower?" asked Rose. "Maybe the box fell off."

They searched on the ground below, but the box wasn't there, either.

Class was over by now. Marigold asked the other fairies if they had seen the box, explaining what she and Rose thought had happened to Flash.

"Whoa," said Poppy. "I bet *he* was surprised when he saw Rose's wand aiming straight at him!"

Rose squirmed. Marigold could guess how her friend must be feeling—as embarrassed as Marigold felt when her brain froze in class. She gave Rose's hand a quick squeeze. "It was an accident," she said. "Any one of us could've done it."

None of the fairies had seen the box. "Poor Flash," said Heather. "Do you think he *knows* he's a box?"

Marigold shuddered. "I hope not." But she couldn't help wondering the same thing. Had Flash felt comforted—as she had—when she'd slept with her arm around him last night?

During lunch Marigold barely touched the large slice of poppy-seed cake Bink served her. While the other fairies spoke in soft voices, she stared into her teacup, thinking sadly about Flash. She'd come so close to having him back and now he had vanished again!

"Still not eating, huh?" Bink asked when he came to clear away the dishes. Marigold and Rose were the only ones yet at the table. The other fairies had finished eating and quietly flown up to the balcony to get ready for their next class.

Marigold shook her head and sighed.

Bink brushed back the lock of reddish-brown hair that was always falling over one eye. "Wait here," he said. "I have something special for you that I think will cheer you up." He hurried to the kitchen and returned in just a moment with a clumsily wrapped package.

"Cookies," Bink said proudly. "I made them myself." He set the package on the table. "You can eat them later, when you start to feel better."

"Thank you," said Marigold. Bink meant well, but the only thing that would make her feel better would be if Flash suddenly appeared.

"Well, aren't you going to open it?" Bink asked.

"Of course," said Marigold politely. It was sweet of Bink to want to cheer her up. For his sake, she'd try to manage a bite or two of at least one cookie.

Marigold unwrapped the paper from around the package and gasped. "The box!" she cried.

"I hope you don't mind that I borrowed it," said Bink. "I saw it lying empty on top of your flower. I wanted to make you feel better by filling it with something good."

Leaping up, Marigold hugged Bink. "You've just given me the best gift ever!"

Bink scratched his head. "It's only cookies."

"Maybe not," said Rose. Pulling out her silver wand, which sparkled with rubies, she tapped the box three times.

Instantly, it vanished. Cookies flew across the table, most of them landing in pieces on the floor. But where was Flash? Then a green light flickered and the firefly crawled out from beneath the table.

"Flash!" cried Marigold. "You're okay!"

His wings made a whirring sound, and then he bobbed his head as if to say, "Of course!"

Bink scratched his head again. "Flash was inside the box?"

"Actually," said Rose sheepishly, "he *was* the box. I accidentally transformed him." She gazed at the firefly. "I'm so sorry, Flash. I didn't mean to mistake you for a twig."

Flash blinked his light on and off.

"He forgives you," said Marigold. She reached out to Flash, and he nuzzled his head against her hand.

Bink stared at the cookie mess on the floor. "Oh, dear," he said sadly. "I'm afraid they're ruined."

"Thanks anyway," said Marigold. "It's the thought that counts." To tell the truth, Bink wasn't a very good baker. The cookies had looked rather burned. Marigold was more than a little relieved that now she wouldn't *have* to eat them.

Rose fluttered her wings. "We've got to let everyone know that Flash is back!"

"Let's bring him with us," said Marigold. "I don't think Mistress Lily will mind if Flash visits class just this once."

9

A Celebration

Flash flew between Marigold and Rose as they fluttered up to the balcony. There were shouts and cheers when the fairies caught sight of the firefly. They all crowded around him.

Mistress Lily smiled. "So this is Flash," she said warmly. "Welcome back." She patted the top of his head. "Aren't you handsome!"

Flash flickered his light on and off rapidly.

Marigold grinned. "He likes what you said."

"I guess you found the box," said Poppy.

"Box?" repeated Mistress Lily.

Rose told the story of her mistake all over again. "I wish I'd taken a closer look before I aimed my wand. Then I would've *seen* it wasn't a twig on that rail."

Mistress Lily smiled. "We often learn more from our mistakes than from the things we do perfectly."

Marigold thought about that. Her misshapen vase had taught her to get a clear picture in her head of what she wanted to create. And though her cookie jar hadn't been perfect, at least it was an improvement over the vase!

"Where did you find the box?" asked Daisy.

Marigold explained how Bink had borrowed it and filled it with cookies. "He didn't know it was Flash, of course."

"We're just glad he's back," said Mistress Lily. "How did you know you'd turned him into a box, Rose?"

"I didn't," she admitted. "It was Marigold who figured it out. Isn't she clever?"

Marigold couldn't believe it! Her best friend—the cleverest fairy she knew—thought that Marigold was clever too.

"There were clues," said Marigold. She stroked Flash's back as he lay at her feet. "It just took me a while to put them all together." She glanced at Mistress Lily. "Sometimes my brain doesn't work as fast as I'd like it to."

"I know the feeling," said Mistress Lily.

She did? Marigold smiled. "I left Flash on my flower bed yesterday evening before Rose went outside to practice. He must have flown to the bridge." She patted his head. "He might have been looking for me.

Or perhaps he just wanted to look at the jewels on the rails. He really likes them." Flash nuzzled her hand as if to say he was sorry for leaving her flower, but glad she understood.

"The box itself was a big clue," said Marigold. "Like Flash, it was oval-shaped. And it matched his colors."

Mistress Lily laid her hand on Marigold's shoulder. "Flash's disappearance was a real puzzle. You did a great job of solving it!"

Marigold beamed.

During the rest of class, Flash stayed close to Marigold's side. Perhaps he was afraid she might disappear the moment he took his eyes off her. "It's okay, Flash," Marigold whispered. "I'm not going anywhere, and neither are you—not without me, anyway."

At the end of class, Mistress Lily said, "How about a dance tonight? You've all been working very hard. And we can celebrate Flash's return."

"Hooray!" shouted the fairies.

After dinner that evening, everyone helped get things ready. Poppy and Daisy cleared the cushions from the sitting area to make room for dancing. Mistress Lily set up her harp. Violet found some colorful streamers and cast a spell to make them float in the air above the dance floor. And the triplets made a banner that said, "Welcome back, Flash" in glittering baby-blue letters.

When it came time to dress for the dance, Rose added elegant touches to everyone's gowns, and Marigold did all the fairies' wings to match their dresses. She even decorated Flash's wings—with red sparkles and white stars. He was pleased with how they looked and flew from fairy to fairy so that everybody could admire them.

To begin the dance, Mistress Lily played "The Fairy Reel." As the fairies twirled around the room, Flash wove between them, his light gaily flashing.

The fairies danced for hours, but at last it was time for bed. Flash was so tired, Marigold and Rose had to carry him between them as they flew outside to the garden. The two fairies settled Flash onto Marigold's flower, then said good night.

"See you in the morning!" Marigold called as Rose flew to her own bed. After changing her gown to pajamas, she snuggled close to Flash. With both of them on top of her flower, it *was* a tight fit, but Marigold didn't think either of them minded.

Flash nuzzled Marigold's cheek, and his

wings whirred softly. Marigold kissed the top of his head. "I love you, too," she said. Now that he was back, it was funny to think that he'd never really been far away—even when he was a box.

Whimsical adventures await at Mistress Lily's Fairy School!

Suzanne Williams

Fairy Blossoms 1

Daisy and the Magic Lesson

Suzanne Williams

Fairy Blossoms 2

Poppy and the Vanishing Fairy

Suzanne Williams

Fairy Blossoms 3

Rose and the Delicious Secret

HarperCollins *Children's* Books   www.harpercollinschildrens.com